Hooked

Hooked

TOMMY GREENWALD

Illustrations by
DAVID McPHAIL

ROARING BROOK PRESS
New York

For Simon Boughton, who has allowed me to write many stories
—T.G.

For Oliver and Harrison, two amazing fishermen
—D.M.

Thanks to Lauren Tarshis, Nancy Mercado, Claire Dorsett,
and Andrew Arnold for helping make this story a book.
And to David McPhail for making this book beautiful.
—T.G.

Text copyright © 2018 by Tommy Greenwald
Illustrations copyright © 2018 by David McPhail
Published by Roaring Brook Press
Roaring Brook Press is a division of Holtzbrinck Publishing Holdings Limited Partnership
175 Fifth Avenue, New York, NY 10010
mackids.com

Library of Congress Control Number: 2017944503
ISBN: 978-1-59643-996-2

Our books may be purchased in bulk for promotional, educational, or business use.
Please contact your local bookseller or the Macmillan Corporate and Premium Sales Department
at (800) 221-7945 ext. 5442 or by e-mail at MacmillanSpecialMarkets@macmillan.com.

First edition, 2018
Book design by Andrew Arnold
Printed in China by Toppan Leefung Printing Ltd., Dongguan City, Guangdong Province

1   3   5   7   9   10   8   6   4   2

Joe loved fishing,
even though nothing much happened.

He would wait.

He would look at the water.

He would look at
the sky.
He would wait
some more.

And he would dream about
catching The Big One.

Joe's dad thought fishing was boring.
"I like more action," he said.
"And I don't like worms."

He just didn't get it.

So Joe joined the town
fishing club.
They fished in streams,
ponds, rivers, and brooks.

One time they even
fished in a puddle.

As Joe grew to love fishing even more, he
asked his dad to give it a chance.
"You should try it!" Joe said.
"No, thank you," his dad answered.

Then one winter day, the leader of Joe's fishing club announced that they were going ice fishing on a frozen lake.

Everyone cheered!

"On this trip, each child must be accompanied by a parent or guardian," the club leader said.

Uh-oh, thought Joe.

That night at dinner, Joe asked his dad
if he would take him ice fishing.
His dad thought for a minute.
"I'll go on one condition," he said.
"What's that?" Joe asked.

Joe's dad smiled. "That I never have
to do it again."

The next Saturday, they woke up very early and drove to the lake.

It was bright and beautiful and twelve degrees.

Joe smiled at his dad.

His dad tried to smile back.

First they carved a round hole in the ice.
Then they dropped in their lines.

Nothing much happened.

They waited.
They looked at the ice.
They looked at the sky.
They waited some more.

Then Joe and his dad
started to talk.

They talked about everything: baseball, movies, music, food, school, animals, and a bunch of other stuff.

They told jokes.
They drank hot chocolate.
But they didn't catch anything.

When the sun began to go down,
they stopped talking.
Joe's dad started shivering.
And Joe started worrying.

He worried that maybe it wasn't a good idea to bring his dad fishing after all.

He worried that his dad might hate fishing now more than ever.

Then, just before it was time to go, Joe felt a tug on his line.

He jumped up.

"I got a bite!" Joe yelled.

Joe's dad tried to jump up, too, but he slipped and fell.

The fish pulled back hard.
It felt big and strong!

Finally, after one last tug, Joe reeled it in.

At first, Joe couldn't tell what kind of fish it was.
Then he realized it wasn't a fish at all.
It was something large, soggy, and pink.
It was . . .

. . . a stuffed elephant.

Everyone started laughing.
Joe's ears burned with
embarrassment.

He started to throw the elephant
back in the lake.

"Don't!" said his dad.

"But it's a stupid stuffed
elephant!" Joe said.

His dad looked at him.

"You caught her," he
said, "and we're
keeping her."

On the way home, Joe and his dad talked about the freezing cold, and drinking hot chocolate, and getting a tug on the line, and Joe's dad falling on his fanny, and Joe catching the stuffed elephant.

They laughed the whole way.

When they got home, Joe's dad put the elephant in the washer and dryer.

It came out warm and fluffy.

"She's adorable," Joe's dad said. "Let's name her Ella."

A few weeks later, when it was time for Joe's first fishing trip of the spring, his dad knocked on his door.

"Can I come with you?" he asked.

Joe and his dad caught only one fish
that day—a little striper they threw back.
   But that didn't matter.
   They talked, and laughed, and had a great time.
   The next time Joe went fishing, his dad went
with him again.

And he went the time after that.
And the time after that.
It turned out Joe's dad loved fishing almost
as much as Joe did.
You could say he was hooked.

And that's how Joe caught The Big One.